W9-CLJ-394

Let's Learn All We Can!

P. K. Hallinan

ideals children's books.
Nashville, Tennessee

First printing this edition 2002

ISBN 0-8249-5449-1

Published by Ideals Children's Books
An imprint of Ideals Publications
A division of Guideposts
535 Metroplex Drive, Suite 250
Nashville, Tennessee 37211
www.idealsbooks.com

Copyright © 1999 by Patrick K. Hallinan

All rights reserved. No part of this publication may be reproduced or
transmitted in any form or by any means, electronic or mechanical,
including photocopy, recording, or any information storage and retrieval
system, without permission in writing from the publisher.

Printed and bound in Mexico by R.R. Donnelley.

Library of Congress Cataloging-in-Publication Data on file.

For Renee Masters, who has taught so many
You Are Smarter Than You Think
—P. K.

Books by P. K. Hallinan

A Rainbow of Friends

For the Love of Our Earth

Heartprints

How Do I Love You?

I'm Thankful Each Day!

Just Open a Book

Let's Learn All We Can!

My Dentist, My Friend

My Doctor, My Friend

My First Day of School

My Teacher's My Friend

That's What a Friend Is

Today Is Christmas!

Today Is Easter!

Today Is Halloween!

Today Is Thanksgiving!

Today Is Valentine's Day!

Today Is Your Birthday!

We're Very Good Friends, My Brother and I

We're Very Good Friends, My Father and I

We're Very Good Friends, My Grandma and I

We're Very Good Friends, My Grandpa and I

We're Very Good Friends, My Mother and I

We're Very Good Friends, My Sister and I

When I Grow Up

10 9 8 7 6 5 4 3 2 1

"Learning is fun!"
Said P. K. to Ben.
"It's all just a matter of
Try, try again!"

"I like learning too,"
Jay quickly agreed.
"I'm happy to know
How to spell and to read."

And Jeannie chimed in,
"I completely agree!
If we learn all we can,
We'll be smart as can be!"

So the kids got together
And made a new rule:
They'd try to apply
Their best efforts at school.

"It's a great thing to do!"
Said Henry to Sue.

In class the next morning
They sat without talking
Then followed instructions—
No groaning or balking.

They asked a few questions
By raising their hands
And asked them again
If they didn't understand.

And none was too shy
To say, "How, when, or why?"

They added their numbers.
They practiced their letters.
They wrote a short sentence—
The neater, the better.

They worked nice and slowly,
At just the right pace
Then giggled a bit
At all they'd erased.

"Learning," laughed Ben,
"Is try, try again!"

They probed into science.

They peered into art.

They delved into music
And singing in parts.

They pondered the planets
That circled the sun
Then drew constellations
Of stars, just for fun.

They worked on computers
And downloaded files.

They searched like researchers
For bugs in the wild.

They even discovered
How long, long ago
Dinosaurs traveled
The plains to and fro!

And high in the sky
Pterodactyls flew by!

They practiced their soccer
As never before,
Because physical fitness
Means more than the score.

And as Jay explained,
"Hey, it's only a game!"

At home they did homework
With gusto and glee.
At school the next day,
They were sharp as could be.

"Learning is great!"
Said Jeannie to Jay.
"I'm going to learn
A bit more every day!"

And Henry concurred,
"That's a really good plan!

Let's give school our best . . .
"Let's learn all we can!"